MW01100326

AROUND ME

For Mom

Copyright © 1992 by Erica Magnus Thomas. All rights reserved. No part of this book may
be reproduced or utilized in any form or by any means, electronic or mechanical, including
photocopying and recording, or by any information storage and retrieval system, without
permission in writing from the Publisher. Inquiries should be addressed to Lothrop, Lee
& Shepard Books, a division of William Morrow & Company, Inc., 1350 Avenue of the
Americas, New York, New York 10019. Printed in Singapore.
First Edition 1 2 3 4 5 6 7 8 9 10

Library of Congress Cataloging in Publication Data   Magnus, Erica. Around me / Erica
Magnus.   p.   cm.   Summary: A child comes to appreciate that even though the world
is large it is still within her reach. ISBN 0-688-09756-1.—ISBN 0-688-09753-7 (lib. bdg.)
I. Title. PZ7.M2737Ar 1991 [E]—dc20   90-26459   CIP   AC

ERICA MAGNUS

AROUND ME

LOTHROP, LEE & SHEPARD BOOKS   NEW YORK

Look at this! The world's so big,

and even so, it fits me.

Tree after tree can grow for miles

inside my sandbox kingdom.

Above my head in all the sky,
a single cloud that's floating by

is still within my reach.

The wind makes waves upon the ground,
the world spins round,

the sun goes down.

And even the most frightening things

are tamed by time

and space.